BUILT

The Mountain Man's Babies

FRANKIE LOVE

COPYRIGHT

❤❤❤❤

JOIN FRANKIE LOVE'S
MAILING LIST
AND NEVER MISS A RELEASE!

And find Frankie on FB!
https://www.facebook.com/
groups/FrankieLoveBooks/

Edited by
ICanEdit4U
Peppermint Editing

ABOUT THE BOOK

BUILT: The Mountain Man's Babies

When I pull into the diner of this small
mountain town, there's only one thing I want.
To put down roots and find someone to build a
life with.
And the woman who pours me a cup of joe is
sweet as sugar and warm as apple pie.
She serves me up a "Josie Special" and I know
she's made to order—the only woman for me.
My past is dark, too dark for a ray of light
like her.
But she cracks open the clouds and lets the
sunshine in ... she sees me as the man I can
become.
Her father wants me gone.
He thinks he knows all about me.
But he's wrong, and I'll do whatever I can to
clear my name.

For Josie. For our love.
For the life we will build together.

———

Dear Reader,
You're going to melt when you meet Beau Montgomery
—he's BUILT, if you know what I mean. He's all man,
all alpha—and all yours. This mountain is full of
babies, and he's gonna make one fine baby-daddy
—guaranteed!
xo, frankie

———

BUILT is a stand-alone story in a sexy world of
mountain men and the women they love.

CHAPTER ONE

Beau

*T*hey say things get harder before they get easier and ain't that the mother fucking truth.

A week out of prison and I'm still trying to reconcile the man I was with the man I am now. I hardly remember what it means to stand under a sky full of stars and look to the heavens and take in a deep breath of air.

For five years, I sat behind bars for a crime I didn't commit; my prison cell containing the parts of me I wanted to leave behind but couldn't. It was like I was carrying a ghost with me the entire stint, but now?

Now, I'm a free man.

I walked through the prison gate and didn't look back. Got my old Scout International from the garage of a guy I used to know--Stan. I could trust him because he wasn't the one who framed me. Tommy is.

When I got my truck, Stan said word was Tommy had been looking for me; wanted to kill me before I could get to him. Guess Tommy thinks I'm pissed at him for what he did.

But being in prison didn't make me angry. It just put things in fucking perspective. I want a life that means something, and murdering Tommy won't get me what I want. Not even close.

Still, Stan said I oughta get the hell out of town to avoid that crazy fucker. I have no intention of getting blood on my hands. Not now. Not ever. So I started driving.

I had no destination in mind, I just knew I needed to get out of Boise. Although we're in Idaho--and the cities here aren't like they are in some shit show like NYC or LA--it's still more than a country boy like me wants. I grew up in the mountains, and the mountains are where I need to be now.

Hell, I've been dreaming of starting my life over in a quiet place. Maybe build myself a house with my own two hands and live a life I can be fucking proud of. I'm not interested in some big and overly ambitious life. My deepest desire is to live a life with someone who will always have my back, through thick and thin.

Someone who won't walk away when things get hard. A woman I can protect and take care of. The last thing I want is to head back to a city where people have forgotten what it means to be a real man.

Who knows? Maybe I'll find her one of these days. But God knows, I won't settle for less.

I have two hands and an able body. I know I'll find work sooner or later. For now, I'm gonna keep driving until there's something worth stopping for. Sleeping in the bed of my truck with the moon overhead at night suits me just fine. And as I drive with the windows down, the cool air covers me with the distinct peace that comes with not being chained down by any man.

I stop on the side of the highway and help a couple with a flat tire. When I tell the older woman that I'm starved, she tells me there's a little diner thirty miles east and it has the best service she's seen in decades.

Taking her advice, I drive the way she suggested and stop at the little diner.

Sliding into a corner booth, I exhale slowly for the first time in days, as I look out the big window. This sleepy mountain vista is the kind of place I picture myself settling down in.

A woman with a nametag reading Rosie,

hands over a menu and offers me a bright smile. A smile that puts me at ease and tells me I came to the right place.

"Morning, darling. Coffee?"

"Sure thing," I tell her as she pours me a steaming mug from a carafe. My eyes widen as a waitress comes through the front doors, tying an apron around her waist. The whole room seems to brighten as she walks in. Her blond ponytail seems to bounce as she walks and she wears a green blouse. She looks like a sunflower; her face turns toward the sun.

Sweet Lord, this is the woman of my goddamn dreams.

She greets the other patrons as she passes them, and Rosie gives her a little wave before turning back to me.

"Josie will help you with your order. She's taking over for me, okay?"

"No problem." I bring the mug to my lips and take a drink. The coffee is good, rich and dark, and once again I thank my lucky stars that I got out of the slammer for good behavior. I've always worked hard and kept my head down, but the fact I was wrongfully imprisoned could have put a chip on my shoulder.

Still, I knew there were two choices when I was behind bars. Get my shit together or get shit on. I knew where I wanted to end up.

And as this sweet-as-sugar waitress walks toward me with an order pad in hand, I thank God I kept my chin up. Getting out early means I'm sitting here right now, with a view like this.

I wouldn't trade this seat for another anywhere in the goddamn world.

"What are you smiling about?" she asks, her voice gentle and warm as she holds a pen over her pad to take my order. She looks down at me, and then she falters for a second. I see it in her eyes. It's like she's looking at me for the first time and realizing I'm not what she expected.

And that she likes what she sees.

Hell, her face is flushed, and she licks her lip, totally unaware of her actions and what they are doing to my cock, luckily hidden under the table.

I don't know much about her except her name, but I know she likes what she sees. Maybe I'm just hyper-aware, having been away from women for so long, but it's like she can sense what I'm feeling and yearning for just by looking at me.

As if she knows how badly I'm longing for a woman to wrap her arms around me and hold me tightly. How badly I'm craving a woman's gentle touch, her warm skin next to mine, her feminine beauty etching new memories in my heart.

And so, when she asks what I'm smiling about, I have no problem telling her the whole truth and nothing but the truth. So, help me, God.

"I'm smiling because I'm sitting here looking at you."

She shakes her head, grinning despite her best effort to suppress the grin.

The guys a few booths over seem to have heard my words. A tall guy with tattoos covering his forearms turns and looks at me.

I look back at the waitress, and right under the logo for Rosie's Diner is her name tag which reads Josie. I smile at that. There's both a Rosie and a Josie working here.

"You flirting with my girl?" the man asks.

Josie scoffs, putting her hands on her hips and giving him a piece of her mind. "I am not your girl, Jonah. I think I've made that crystal clear by now."

The guy next to Jonah jabs him with his elbow. "Cut it out. Let Josie have some fun."

The guy, Jonah, scoffs. "I know, I'm just giving her a hard time. I can do that, I'm her best friend."

I watch the dynamics between these people. The group of five men in their flannel shirts, all with thick beards, clearly a group of hard-working guys. And I'm just trying to figure out how Josie fits into the group.

She looks down at me. "Don't worry about him. Jonah is my best friend and gets territorial."

I lean closer and the soft lavender perfume she wears makes me dizzy. I knew I wanted to find a real woman after I left the slammer. However, I didn't expect to find her so damn fast.

"Oh yeah? Is he my competition?" I ask with a smirk. I'm not going to beat around the bush here. I want her.

"Not at all. We tried that. But we're staying in the friend zone."

The guys at the table break out in laughter over this, Jonah shaking his head in a fake scowl. It's clear he agrees with this, though. From what I can tell, Josie has a lot of men in her corner, and I'm glad for that. A woman as gorgeous as her needs people around who have her back.

"Girl," he says to Josie. "You gotta stop busting my balls. I got a reputation to uphold."

She snickers. "Your reputation was trashed long before me."

I appreciate that she's laying this all out for me from the get-go. She's making it clear that she is on the market. As in *not taken*.

"Look," I say to Jonah. "I wasn't doing anything but making conversation."

Josie pipes up. "Well, then that's a crying shame."

The guys bust up laughing again and I grin. This woman is letting me know exactly where she stands.

"So, what can I get you, stranger?" she asks, straightening her shoulders and doing her best to look professional. "I've got a Josie Special or a to-die-for stack of flapjacks."

"I'll take your special."

"Do you wanna know about the special?" she asks.

"If it's got your name on it, I'm guessing it's good."

She doesn't miss a beat. Licking her lips, she slowly says, "It's delicious."

"Good. Because like I said, that's what I want."

"You know what you want before you even know what it is?" She taps her pen on the pad, and I look her up and down. Narrow waist, curvy hips, a pair of tits that could make even the toughest man weak in the knees and hard in the fucking groin.

Five years is a long ass time to not have a woman. And she's not just a woman. She is something else entirely.

Mine.

"No doubt about it."

And that's the truth.

"Damn, you're laying it on thick," Jonah says whistling low.

One of the other men raises his eyebrows. "Josie deserves a man who will walk in here and tell her how it is. I like this guy already."

I run a hand over my beard, appreciating these men and how they really care about this woman, and not in some demeaning way, but in a kind of 'we're-looking-out-for-her' way.

The other waitress, Rosie, walks out of the back room with a purse over her shoulder. "Hey Buck, I'm headed out. But don't forget to pick up the prescription for the boys at the pharmacy before you come home tonight. They still have a cough. Okay, baby?" She leans over and kisses one of the men in the booth. He looks at her with devotion as he tells her he won't forget. Josie fixes her gaze on them too, sighing a little as the husband and wife pull apart.

I'm not quite sure who these people are, and what town I ended up in. It seems like some sort of alternative reality--but they all seem like good people. Salt of the earth.

Josie turns back to me. "So, you want the special then?"

I nod. That's exactly what I want.

CHAPTER TWO

Josie

I walk back to the kitchen and give the order to the cook. Then I step out through the back door and sit down on the steps to catch my breath.

That man is *built*. Ruggedly handsome and his southern accent has me all flustered. All my lady parts are on fire and my throat is parched. He was burning me up from the inside out and I don't even know his name.

It's a long time since I had a man.

Okay, it's been basically forever. I moved to this mountain a little over a year ago to help my granddaddy during the last year of his life. He passed away months ago and now it's just me in his big old house.

Besides this job, I hang out with my new girlfriends, Rosie, Harper, Grace, Cherish, and

Honor. A better group of women do not exist. All of us have our own quirks and personalities, but the common thread here is community.

All the women are happily married with more children than any of us can count. Except for Grace and me. We're still waiting to meet our untamed mountain men.

And there hasn't been any fresh man meat on this mountain for a *long* time.

Everyone pushed Jonah and me together for a while, but after a few dates, it was clear that we weren't meant to be like *that*. Best friends, sure. Lovers? Not a chance.

He's still a little too wild for me. I want a man who knows what he wants and how he wants it. I have no interest in a man who is still trying to figure out who he wants to be and why.

And so far, that man hasn't come knocking on my door.

But that's okay, I busied myself with my granddad and now that he's gone--God rest his soul--I spend more time with everyone's babies, helping my friends out.

My dad has called repeatedly, hinting that I should come back home now that Granddad is gone. He thinks I should return to Boise, but there's something about this mountain that keeps me here.

Something about it makes me feel grounded. Rooted.

And now that Granddad has left me his place, the last thing I want to do is walk away from the life I've created for myself.

Even if it a far cry from what everyone expected from me.

My old city friends are like my dad--they just don't understand. They wonder why I'm here at all. There aren't any dance clubs or flashy bars that twenty-four-year-old women should apparently be frequenting.

But there are friends and family. A real community.

That is more than enough. It's everything I never knew I wanted.

My waitressing job may seem simple to my old friends who are working on second degrees to become attorneys or doctors but it feels good to put food on a table or to refill someone's mug of coffee and give a smile that I know will make someone's day.

I stand from the back steps, having regained my composure and walk back into the diner. I know who I am and I know what I want.

And maybe... just maybe... he walked through the doors this morning and asked for my special.

A girl can dream.

I begin clearing the table where Jonah sits. The other guys: Buck, Wilder, James, Hawk, and Jaxon are there too, a table full of men who love deeply and fiercely; who can pick up their baby for a diaper change just as easily as they shoot the shit.

See? This life is more than enough. It's the life I chose.

I choose to believe that there's more for me on this mountain yet.

The man who made my body tingle from head to toe watches me as I clear the guys' table.

As I reach for their breakfast plates, Buck asks how my granddad's house is doing. Everyone knows it's a work in progress.

"You know what it needs. And actually, I was going to talk to you guys about it. My father sent me some extra money to get some of the projects done."

"Oh, yeah? That's good of him," Jax says. They all know how my father has reservations about me living here; but he still wants me to be happy. My father is the best man I know. He's a well-honored judge but still respects my choices even though he doesn't agree with them. So, the fact he's financially helping me to fix up Grand-dad's place means a lot.

"The kitchen needs to be remodeled, but

the more pressing thing is the porch. It's ruined after that winter we just had. Do you think you could spare someone from your crew to take a look at it?"

Buck and Jaxon share a look. "I don't know how soon we can get to it, Josie," Buck says. "We're finishing up those houses off old Christianson Road and all hands are on deck right now. Think you could wait about a month?"

"Sure," I tell him. Of course, I really want the front steps finished sooner, but it's not the worst thing to have to go through the back entrance. Still, I really wanted to start out Spring with me drinking cups of coffee on that front porch every morning, looking up at the mountain above me and the trees around me.

I know it's a silly thing to dream of having. The perfect place for a cup of morning coffee, especially when a few minutes later, I'll be driving down to the diner to pour cups all day long.

But still, I was hoping to get at least one house project started sooner rather than later.

Jaxon must notice my disappointment because he says, "I wish another guy would come our way. Just hard find anyone these days. It's as if guys just want a job where they can sit behind a computer screen and telecommute."

"Agreed," says Buck. "What we need are real

men. Men who know how to work with their hands, who aren't just interested in iPhone apps, but want to make something with a hammer and nails."

I smile and reach for the coffee pot to refill their mugs. Get these boys on a roll about hard work and ethics, and I'll be here all day.

"Okay, boys. Well, in that case, you better get off your tushes and get to work yourselves."

As they finish their mugs of java, I drop off the dirty pile of dishes, make a fresh pot of coffee, grab the special from the orders-up counter, and head back to my new favorite customer.

"Here you go, stranger," I say with a smile.

"And now that it's here, what is this special, exactly?" he asks looking down at the plate of goodness. "I don't think I would have ordered something so... delicate."

"They are crepes. And I promise you'll love them." I lick my lips. "Whipped cream and honey-filled crepes."

"With berries on top?" He asks with a flirtatious smile.

"Cherries, actually."

"How did you know what my dreams were made of?" he asks with a groan.

I shake my head, knowing if I keep talking

about his breakfast, I will push it all off the table and attempt to ravish him.

Death by sweet cream.

"So," I say, fanning myself with a menu. "I don't think I caught your name."

"It's Beau. Beau Montgomery."

His words are slow and steady, and they make my heart beat fast just to hear them. And that southern drawl has me drooling.

"I'm Josie. "

"Figured as much," he says pointing to my nametag. "So, you're looking for an extra hand to work on your house?"

"I am," I say refilling his coffee as he takes a bite of my special. "So, were you overhearing or eavesdropping?" I smile. I'm not exactly good at flirting, but this is Beau Montgomery.

With dreamy eyes and thick eyelashes that make my knees jelly. For him, I'm interested in getting a heck of a lot better at it.

"Overhearing." He shrugs. "And I was wondering maybe I could get an introduction to those men?"

"Of course," I say. Then I call over Jaxon and Buck, the owners of the local construction company.

"Jax, Buck, this is Beau Montgomery and he wanted to talk to you about some work." I look at Beau to make sure I had it right.

Through some non-verbal man cues--chin juts and raised eyebrows--Jax and Buck slide into the booth across from Beau and they start talking about job history and experience.

I head back to the kitchen to drop off some empty plates and peer through the kitchen door watching as Jaxon and Buck get into a conversation with Beau. At one point, Hawk joins them and then they're all nodding in agreement over something.

After the guys leave, I head back to see Beau pulling out his wallet.

"So, how did it go?" I ask not wanting to be too nosy but wanting to know everything.

"Thanks for the introduction, Josie. They offered me a trial job."

"Really?" My eyes widen. "Are you from around here?"

"No, but I've been looking for a place to put down some roots. This place looks as good as any."

I shake my head. "No, this place is certainly not as good as any. It's the best place I've ever been."

"You been to many places, Josie?" He looks at me as if he's looking deep inside my heart; as if he can see the burning desire crawling up my skin. Something about this man draws me to him. That makes me want what is mine for the taking.

"Not as many as I'd like."

"Wanna go somewhere?" he asks.

"What did you have in mind?" I ask, sitting down across from him. The gravitational pull so damn strong.

"I have a truck, I can take you anywhere you like, Josie."

"Thought you just got a new job?" I cross my arms and tease. "Already wanting to ditch out on that gig?"

He twists his lips, runs a hand through his hair. "Nah, I don't want to run. I want to settle down, build something meant to last."

The energy between us intensifies, how did we get to this so quickly? Before I can reach my arms around his neck and mount him here in the diner, Jaxon walks back to the table.

"Okay," Jaxon says, "I spoke to my buddy James and he says it's good with him."

"What's good? I ask, not minding my own business.

Jaxon looks at me as if he knows what I'm up to. "I asked James if he was all right with us borrowing his old trailer for a while."

"His camper?"

"Yeah," Jaxon says. "We're gonna give Beau

here a trial run. He is looking for a place to settle down for a while. Ain't that right, son?"

I half roll my eyes at Jaxon, acting like some old man on the mountain when he's really only thirty-six. Though I'm guessing he's ten years older than Beau.

"That's right sir," Beau says.

"James will bring the trailer down the mountain tonight, alright? We'll park it in the empty lot here behind the diner. Right now, you can head over to Josie's place with me and we can check out her porch. Then if the job is something you can handle, you can work there today, sound good?"

"You won't regret it," Beau says, standing from the table. Jax claps him on the back and both men tell me good-bye.

I wish Beau could stay longer, like until my lunch break, perhaps. But I have a four-hour shift to finish up. It kills me to watch him go. I'm wishing Beau could stay here all day.

And with naughty thoughts filling my mind, I think about staying with him all night too.

I watch the men get up to leave, thinking that if I'm lucky Beau will be at my place when I get off work. Beau turns before he reaches the front door, and offers me a wink. "I'll be seeing you soon, Ms. Josie," he tells me.

I clear his table, picking up the money and

bill, noticing he wrote something on it before leaving.

J,

*   Hoping I'll be able to enjoy another Josie's Special sometime soon.*

*   B.*

I bite my bottom lip, rereading the note, already making plans.

I will certainly give him a Josie's special tonight as a thank you gift for fixing up my porch.

And that special won't be crepes. It will be something else entirely.

CHAPTER THREE

Beau

I'm wiping the sweat from my forehead when Josie pulls into the driveway mid-afternoon. Buck left a few minutes ago, wanting to make sure I was doing what I said I'd do. I appreciate that they checked in on me. After all, I am just a stranger and this is their town, their community. And hell, I told him I'd just got out of the slammer. The fact they trust me means a helluva lot.

Josie is in a little SUV and when she steps out, her face lights up.

"You're here."

I stand, setting down the nail gun and nod slowly, not trusting myself to say anything, because what I'd say would wipe that sweet smile straight off her face. My thoughts are dirty, devious. After spending the last few hours here, outside her home, all I've been thinking about is carrying her up to her bedroom, untying her little apron, and telling her it was high time I placed another order.

"So Jax trusted you with this job?" She saunters toward me and I'm disappointed for a second to see the apron has already come off. But then I realize it is just one less thing to get rid of before I have my way with her.

I may be getting a little ahead of myself, but damn, this woman has consumed me from the moment we met. I know what I want.

"Do you like what you see?" I ask, watching as she inspects the progress. I have a saw set up on a plank of wood that rests on a pair of sawhorses. The green grass is covered in sawdust, and a pile of rotten wood has been tossed aside after I ripped up the old flooring.

"This is amazing," she says peering over the edge of the porch. I removed the steps, so she can't get up to inspect my work. "You ready for a break? Looks like you could use a beer."

I run a rag over my neck, wiping the sweat there and nod, my cock tightening at the prospect of spending some time with her, alone, and I follow her around the house to the back door.

"The house is really old," she says. "But my Granddad loved this place. And I loved him.

I'm a sucker for nostalgia. He died this year and left the place to me." She opens the door and I follow her into the kitchen. "Oh, I bet Jax told you all that."

"He filled me in," I say looking around the vintage kitchen. "Sorry about your granddad."

"Thanks. He was sick for a long time, and I know he was in a lot of pain. Still, I miss him of course. And this spring I'll miss the sound of his old tv blaring the baseball scores. Or the giant zucchini from his garden that he never picks soon enough. I'll miss the way he always had a pitcher of sun tea in the fridge, always ready to pour me a glass." Josie bites her bottom lip, shaking her head. "Sorry," she says. "Guess I'm a sucker for good memories, too."

"Don't apologize," I tell her. "I can't recall ever meeting my grandparents, so I think you're really lucky, Josie."

"Thanks," she says. "But this place he left me is due for a massive overhaul. I want a classic farmhouse kitchen with an apron sink, the hard-wood floors refinished, the claw foot bathtub re-enameled. I want it to look straight out of a 1940's photograph."

I look around, trying to see what she sees. "This house has tons of character, but I can see why you want it renovated."

The appliances look thirty years old, the

linoleum floor is broken in places, and the Formica countertops are peeling.

"Yeah, it's a big project. Do you see this wallpaper?" she asks smiling. The walls are covered in 70's mushrooms and orange and yellow leaves.

"What else did Jaxon say when he showed you around?"

"He said not to do anything stupid when it came to you."

"He's always trying to act like my big brother." She reaches in the fridge and grabs two beers. I take them from her and pop off the bottle tops with my hand, giving her one back. We raise our beers, then take a sip, as we head back outside.

"Have you known him long?" I ask as she leads me to a side garden where there are a few chairs set up around a fire pit.

"Oh, just a little over a year or so." She tells me how she moved here to help with her granddad but fell in love with the town and the people. How everyone here seems to have a half a dozen babies and how she helps the women out as often as she can, because, according to her, babies are the cutest things ever.

Her words, not mine.

We sit, drinking our beer, and she cocks her

head to the side. "Sorry. Do I sound baby crazy?"

I laugh. "Naw. Sounds like you found a pretty perfect place to settle down though."

She laughs too, the sound of her voice filling the blue sky. Looking at her makes me wonder how I ended up here at all. She is fresh air and sun rises and the last five years of my life have been nothing but concrete and restrictions. She is the breath of life I need; the oxygen my body craves.

"What about you?" she says, leaning back in the chair. "Why are you out here on your own?"

"It's a sad story."

"Yeah?" Josie leans in, waiting for me to say more.

"Yeah," I take another sip of beer. I already told Jax, Buck, and Hawk most of my story before they agreed to take me on and with good reason. They need to make sure I wasn't a fucking *whatever* and since Hawk had been to jail himself, he gave the other guys his perspective.

Every man needs a second chance.

And I don't exactly want to hash it out again, so soon.

Especially when I know it would scare a woman like Josie. Hell, it would scare any woman. "I never had much family," I tell her.

"Left South Carolina when I was eighteen, a buddy from school had a relative in Idaho who needed some guys for his construction crew, so we moved out together. Building houses and learning the trade."

"And you've been here ever since?"

"Yeah. It's a good place, lots of trees, lots of land. Good people." I smile, running a hand over my beard. "I grew up in a small mountain town, and it's where I feel most at home."

"But I bet you miss shrimp and grits," Josie says with her eyebrows raised.

I give her a slow smile. "What do you know about grits, girl?"

She shrugs. "Not much, to be honest. Went to visit a second cousin once in the south though, and they were crazy about their grits."

"And what are you crazy about, Josie? Besides babies?"

She finishes her beer and sets it down in the gravel. "I'm pretty simple, Beau. I like the diner, making people smile." She twists her lips, thinking. "And my granddad's house, I guess you could say I'm pretty crazy about it."

"A big house for one woman."

She swallows. "Yeah, my dad thinks I should sell it. That I should move back to Boise."

"But you don't wanna?"

She shakes her head. "I don't. I went to

Boise State for college. Got a degree in finance, of all things. But I don't know, a job at a bank seems like my entire existence would be about paying bills and getting by. I'd like to think life could be about more than that."

I nod. This girl and I may come from different places, but somehow, we both ended up here, right now.

In this moment.

And maybe we aren't that different when you look at what matters.

"It's not the worst thing to want a life that not everyone understands, is it?" I ask her.

"No, no it's not." She tilts her head to the side as if gauging me. "And what about you Beau? Do people understand you?"

"Not usually."

"What do they usually think?"

"That I'm the sum of my past mistakes instead of a man who wants to fight for his future."

Her eyes soften, and she looks at me with a tenderness I didn't realize I needed so damn badly. "And your future, you're ready for it?"

"For the last five years, I've been aching to chase whatever life has for me."

She pushes she lips forward, suppressing a smile.

"What?" I ask.

"And all that fighting, it brought you here?"

I nod, standing, and reaching for her hands. We are standing but a foot apart, and I take both her hands in my own and damn, her skin is smooth, and her eyes are bright. She is the sunrise, the dawn I need. A fresh start, a clean slate.

She is a new beginning.

"It did, Josie. It brought me right here."

I look down at her, wanting to risk it all with a kiss, wondering if she's as ready for this as I am.

But I don't have to take any chances because she pulls up on her tiptoes, wrapping her arms around my neck.

She does need this as badly as I do.

Whispering she asks, "Are you hungry for a Josie Special?"

My cock is stiff at her words, at her proximity, with the knowledge that this is going to happen exactly as I dreamed the entire afternoon as I was hammering away on her front porch, picturing her sweet body grinding against me.

"Girl," I groan. "With you in my arms, it's like I've been starving my whole damn life."

Then I kiss her.

CHAPTER FOUR

Josie

*H*is kiss is like a charge of electricity, a lightning rod. A surge of desire where all the lights go out.

Except we're outside, and it's his mouth that is doing this to me. Soft and demanding as his tongue slides into my mouth, finding mine, taunting me with swirls of desire and greedy moments of delight.

This kiss could take out a freaking power grid, it's that powerful. In his arms, I feel like jelly. My balance and perspective and rational mind are long gone. I want him to turn up the voltage and I don't care what kind of watts he is using--I just want to be plugged into him.

Basically: I'm turned the fuck on.

"I don't usually do this," I tell him between kisses.

"Neither do I, Josie," he tells me. "But I want to. Now."

And maybe it's those words, the way he says my name between kisses. The way he tells me so plainly what he wants—me. But I know, right now, that this is really happening.

"Let's go upstairs," I say, lacing my fingers through his, expecting him to follow me, but instead he picks me up and my legs effortlessly wrap around his waist, his hands firmly on my ass, his low growl of desire waking my core.

"Beau," I moan as he carries me upstairs with a need I've never seen in a man before-- primal and intense--but also so damn desperate. He's desperate for me, like I'm the only thing in this world that will calm his wild heart.

Up the stairs, I point to the last room on the left, and he lies me down on a quilt in my four-poster bed. The window is open, the spring breeze wafting through and the honeysuckle plant that blossoms below fills the room with a scent so sweet and pure that I close my eyes, letting the moment and all its incredulity, wash over me.

"When you close your eyes, you look like an angel," he tells me, leaning over my body, his arms on either side of me, pinning me in.

I blink, looking into his soulful baby blues.

"I'm no saint," I tell him. "I've done this before."

"So have I. But girl, never with you."

And it's like all the times of the past just fall away. The stupid high school boys and even more idiotic guys in college. None of them compare to this because the truth of it is, this is the first time I have been kissed by a man.

And Beau Montgomery is *all man*.

He kisses me again, this time with a fire coursing through his skin, consuming me, my lips are swollen, and my pussy is desperate, and I don't know what will happen next but if it compares at all to that kiss--I know it's going to be good.

Besides, you can't kiss like that and not know how to fuck.

He unbuttons my green top, and when he pushes it away my breasts bounce in the sheer bra barely cupping them.

"Damn, you look so good, Josie," he says with that needy look in his eyes--the look he had in the diner when he asked for my special.

I want to make him look like this every day of his life.

He unclasps my bra at the center hook and then my breasts are bare, exposed. But I don't feel vulnerable to him.

I feel beautiful.

"Good God," he groans, kissing my tits, my nipples in his mouth as he sucks them and I run my hands through his thick hair as he touches my breasts with a hungry need I understand.

I need it too.

Then he pulls his shirt over his head, his rock-hard chest coming into view and causing me to sit up, shed my own shirt sleeves, and unabashedly look him over with mouth gaping in desire.

"Beau... you are..." I shake my head. This is not a body you can get by occasionally going to Cross Fit. This is a body that's made from moving, constantly. His six pack is firm, his biceps are bigger than I could encircle with both hands.

He shakes his head, as if not liking the attention, and I'm grateful he isn't one of those asshole dudes who always want to focus on themselves--on their bodies.

He pulls off my jeans, my lacy panties too. And for a split second I feel too exposed, but then he looks me over, from head to toe, while I'm completely naked before him on my bed. And I don't feel naked... I just feel seen.

"Josie, you are perfection."

I shake my head, not wanting to hear it. It's one thing to have sex with a stranger who is good with his hands. At least, in theory. I mean, he does know how to rebuild a porch. It is another thing to have that man tell you that you're perfection.

I can't believe it.

I shake my head, pressing my hands to his lips. "Shhh," I tell him. "Don't say things you don't mean."

He leans back her me. "Maybe you don't know what I mean, yet, Josie. But I'm going to work you over until you believe me. You. Are. Perfection."

And then he unbuckles his belt, stepping out of his jeans and revealing all of himself to me.

I swallow at the sight of his thick cock. It's more than a mouthful; he's a complete meal.

So, this is how these hook-ups work.

I think I had forgotten or maybe bad college dorm sex doesn't count as a real hook-up anyways.

But this is real.

Beau Montgomery, naked before me, is one hundred percent real. He's a red-blooded American and he is ready for me. Throbbing for me.

I feel faint.

"You okay?" he asks as if worried.

"Um, yeah." I clear my throat. Remember to breathe. "I'm more than okay. I'm great."

He walks toward me, stroking himself as he comes nearer to the bed where I'm naked.

"Good," he says gravely. "Because you look a little anxious."

"I'm not. I just. Like I said... it's been awhile."

"It's been a while for me too."

He says that, but I have a sneaking suspicion that his '*a while*' is very different than mine. It's been a few years for me.

And my body knows it.

Suddenly the desire to be with him, right now--this man with a thick rod of pleasure in his hand--overwhelms me.

"You're really big, Beau."

"And you're really wet," he says, running his hand between my thighs, feeling how slick I am for him. His hand presses against my pussy, my clit already needy for him, and as if he can sense this, he dips a finger inside me, against me-- warming me up.

But my body was made primed and ready for him. It's as if all the lust in the world has been brought here to this room, and it covers us in a thick blanket of desire.

Unable to hold back, he leans over me, kissing me again, his mouth needier now. My hand runs over his cock and I stroke his solid shaft, already dreaming of it between my legs, pressed deep inside me until it breaks me in half. Because I already know that after this I will never *be* the same.

This is everything.

"Oh, girl, you feel so good and tight," he growls, his fingers working me over, my pussy throbbing under his touch. "You like that?" he asks.

And I nod, unable to speak because, in truth, I am panting for breath--panting for him. When I come against his hand, I feel my knees buckle. He has finger-fucked me until I'm soaking wet, the bed a mess, and the two of us are just starting.

Just warming up.

I pull myself up, knees apart and he stands between them. I lean my head down, taking his hardness in my mouth. He undoes my ponytail, running his fingers through my hair as I take him. His tip is so smooth, and I swirl my tongue around him, unable to believe that this happening.

But it is. His veiny cock is begging me to take more and I deep throat him, Beau pushing the back of my head, hungry for me.

I will give it to him.

My jaw is tight as I suck him off, moving my tongue over his hard ridges. He groans against me, tugging at my hair as he holds it by fistfuls. And when he comes, I let it slide down my throat as I pump him harder for more of his milky release.

It tastes so good, and yet I need more. I turn over on all fours, as he stands behind me, his growing cock running over my ass. He holds my hips and then he cups my breasts. It's as if he wants to feel me and take me in every way.

I want that too. I want it more. I want it now.

His cock moves against my slick pussy, my body opening to him as he fills my cunt with his solid shaft.

I scream out, clenching the quilt as he fills me in a deep way I've never experienced. He comes at me with full force and I realize it is exactly what I need.

I need to scream his name and beg him to move harder, more, deeper, forever.

He comes in my pussy, my body responding to everything Beau is willing to offer. And as we collapse in my bed, I realize he is willing to give me an awful lot. I roll to face him, our knees touching, our hands on one another's faces as we catch our breath and still our hearts.

"Josie, what kind of miracle worker are you?" he asks, his voice sincere and low. Raw.

"Miracles? I don't have much need for those."

"No?" His eyes search mine. "What do you need?"

I sigh, nestling closer, my body already wanting another go. "If I can trust the person I am with, that is all that matters," I tell him. "And when I look in your eyes, Beau, I trust what I see."

He swallows hard at the words. "What do you see, Josie?"

"I see a man who knows exactly what he wants."

"And can he have it?" he asks in a hoarse whisper.

"Yes," I tell him, pulling him nearer, spending my legs as he pulls himself on top of me. "Yes, Beau Montgomery, you can."

CHAPTER FIVE

Beau

*S*omewhere over the last week, I fell into some vortex where my past no longer is looking to bite me in the ass. I keep thinking Tommy and his cronies will find me, but so far nothing bad has hunted me down.

Instead, I landed on this mountain where people say hello, watch one another's kids, and have BBQs.

I grew up with a drunk father. There were never neighborhood block parties. There were cases of Bud Light and lots of yelling. Rent was always late, the hot water usually out, and my lunch was had on the government's dime.

But this mountain doesn't operate that way. This place is like a fucking Norman Rockwell painting. Red, white, and blue, through and through.

And to say I feel a little out of my element is no joke.

But Josie insists that I belong as much as anyone else.

"Grace and I were over at Harper's and she and Rosie wouldn't drop the topic of you," she tells me. "Then Stella showed up and started in, and next thing I know, Honor and Cherish were there. It was a lot of interrogation."

I give her a sidelong glance as I finish sanding the rails for her porch. "And you think telling me that six women were all talking about me is gonna make me want to go meet them?"

Josie grimaces. "I know. But the food will be good. Rosie makes a mean potato salad. And Cherish is bringing pies."

"I only want what you're serving, Josie," I tell her. Her cheeks redden, my compliments getting her nice and bothered. "How about we have a little nap before the barbecue."

She smirks. "You don't know the first thing about naps, mister."

Nonetheless, she comes up the front steps of her newly finished porch and I follow her inside.

"What kind of nap were you thinking?" I ask, pulling her over my shoulder and spanking her ass while carrying her up the stairs.

I don't know how long this picture-perfect moment in my life will last. Eventually, all good things come to an end. At least for me they always do. But right now, I have a pretty, little thing in my arms and I intend on keeping her to myself for as long as I can.

"A quick nap," she says. "I promised the girls we'd be there at five."

I shut the bedroom door, pinning her to the wall. She squeals in delight as I pull up her skirt and pull down my pants. Against the wall, her tight cunt sinks against my hard cock.

It's impossible to sleep when there is a woman like this in the world.

"You seem nervous," Josie says a while later as I park my Scout in the gravel driveway, next to a bunch of twelve passenger vans.

"I am."

"What, you've never gone home to meet the parents?" she laughs.

When I shake my head, she gives me a wry look. "Well, these friends are the easy part. If you want to keep seeing me, eventually you're gonna have to go to my dad's for dinner."

Damn, I am feeling over my head in a hundred ways right now. Josie's friends are one thing. Her family is another. I just got out of prison, and everyone else in Josie's life has their shit together.

Josie carries a basket of her homemade cornbread as we walk up to Buck's place. The home is beautiful but smaller than his co-owner, Jaxon's place. But all their properties are sprawling. They are practically parks in their own right, with green grass, conifer trees, and large play structures for the kids.

And there are a lot of kids. Josie tried to warn me on the way here, but I swear they are multiplying before my eyes. Two dozen kiddos are running around at all heights and speeds.

"See," Josie says smiling. "Why would anyone leave this place?"

I swallow, trying to man up and make sure I can make Josie proud. We've only spent a week together. This relationship is as new as new can get. And there is still a lot I want to share with Josie. I want to tell her who I am and what my past really looked like.

Where I've been the past five years and why.

The last thing I want to do is scare her away, but at the same time, she deserves to know everything.

Jonah meets us out front and Josie gives him a hug right away. I know there is nothing going on between the two of them, but seeing her with him makes me realize how much I care about her. How I want to be the only man for her.

"Hey, buddy," Buck says as we head to the backyard patio. Josie peels off toward the kitchen and Jonah watches me closely, as if making sure I'm not up to anything shady. He's stopped by the farmhouse a few times this week while I was there working alone, and he gave me a hand. He seems like a good guy, but he's definitely unsure about me. The line of questioning he comes up with makes me think he doubts my story.

The men are standing around the grill, watching meat cook, and the ladies are in the kitchen, laughing and pouring wine. Some of the dads are pushing their kids in swings, and everyone seems to be holding a baby.

It takes my breath away; this town. It's one where everyone truly is looking after one another.

"Can I get you a beer?"

I nod and Buck hands me a cold one. "Homebrewed," he tells me. "We're pretty picky about our beer on this mountain."

I take a drink. "It's really good," I tell him honestly. I swear to God there aren't men like this anywhere else, at least nowhere I've been. They make their own beer, hold their babies because they want to, take care of their wives because they love them.

I swear, I have a man-crush on these guys, and I'm not ashamed to admit it. They fucking know what matters in life.

"How's it going over at Josie's?" Buck asks as he flips BBQ chicken.

"Going well. Though you should know," I say grinning. Truth is, Buck or Jax, or one of the other guys stop by a few times a day to make sure the new guy on the crew is doing his job right. "Finished the porch today. I was looking at the kitchen and the whole thing needs to be gutted. The bones look good though. It would be great if you could spare a few minutes early next week and give me your opinion," I tell him. He says of course straight away.

I genuinely trust his input and don't want to do anything to fuck up what I have going on right now.

I want this to last.

Josie walks out of the kitchen holding a baby with wisps of blond hair. She looks so natural as if a holding an infant was second nature. When a toddler starts fussing at her feet.

"Auntie Josie, I need to go potty!"

She kneels down and says something to him, before calling for Cherish. "I'm gonna take your little one to the bathroom, okay?"

A woman with long blond hair thanks her, and takes the baby from Josie's arms. It's like an orchestrated dance and they all know the moves, never tripping over anyone else's feet. It's fucking beautiful.

Other women bring out bowls of food and platters of fruit. Kids clamber to the picnic tables and the dads all pitch in to get the kids' plates.

I step back watching the scene unfold, not really knowing my place. Eventually though, Josie returns from the bathroom and the adults begin going through the assembly line to fill our own plates with food.

Sitting down with Josie, we find ourselves directly across from Jaxon and Harper.

"So, how are you liking the area?" Harper asks warmly as she dices watermelon for the little one beside her. Jaxon plays with the ends of her hair, and it's obvious he can't keep his hands off his wife.

"The trees, fresh air, the mountains--it's all gorgeous."

Josie reaches under the table and squeezes my hand. "I think I should take him on the East Summit hike this weekend."

"A hike?" I turn to her with raised eyes. "I didn't know you were into that."

"It's gorgeous," she promises. "And I like getting outside when I can."

"It's true," Harper agrees. "Last year, Josie helped with the garden up here."

"You garden too? Man, this community feels a little too good to be true," I admit, spreading butter on my cornbread.

"Is it overwhelming?" Jax asks, picking up a toddler, and sitting him down on his knee.

"Not in a bad way, but man, there is a lot going on."

"Well, Josie is amazing with the kids," Harper says. "She's been so helpful, even when she was going through hard times with her granddad."

"That's what I'm noticing," I tell them.

"And what are your plans, Beau?" Harper asks.

I look over at Josie for guidance, but she just looks at me with interest. Guess I'm taking a stab at this one solo. I look around the table and notice Jonah watching me out of the corner of his eye as he cuts up chicken into tiny pieces on the plate of the toddler next to him.

I thought I'd be in the hot seat tonight and I was right.

"I like the work I'm doing now. I wouldn't mind continuing it."

"Neither would I," Josie says.

I want to tell her so much before her emotions get too wrapped up in me. But as she laces her fingers through mine, I know in my gut that it's already too late.

I should have told her more by now.

Instead, I've told her nothing. Left out the information that's might change the way she sees me. I know it has only been a week, but sometimes a week is longer than five years. Sometimes one week can change your entire life.

"And how is James's trailer working?" Jax asks.

"Real good," I say, glancing over at Josie and noticing the way the word *trailer* makes her blush. Truth is, I haven't spent all that much time in it.

"So, you're gonna be starting demo on Josie's kitchen?" a woman down the table asks. Josie tried to prep me on her friends earlier and I think this one is Stella.

"Yep. Buck is going to come over in the next few days and help with the assessment, but looks like there isn't any reason to begin gutting the place," I tell her.

"If you need any help, Josie, picking out colors or finding cabinets, I know a lot of great vendors for reasonable prices," Stella says.

"That would be awesome," Josie says. "I'm

grateful that my dad is paying to get the place put together right, but I still want to be smart about the renovations. I know there is a ton of other work that needs to be done. The bathrooms are a mess, there is wallpaper in the bedrooms and the wood floors need to be refinished."

"How many bedrooms are there?" Harper asks.

"Four," Josie says.

"Wow, that's a lot of space," Stella says. She has a twinkle in her eye as she adds, "How are you planning on filling all those rooms?"

Josie's blushes even harder and Wilder elbows his wife. "Aww, give them some time to figure things out."

"You're right. Sorry." Stella frowns apologetically before pulling her husband's mouth to her own, giving him a kiss.

Jonah rolls his eyes at the pair before replying with a scowl. "Yeah. It's only been a week. Let's not assume this is going to go down like the rest of your guys' courtships."

James sits beside him and runs a hand over his beard. "Hey, let's keep it cool, man."

Josie shoots Jonah dagger eyes, and then Harper chimes in, "Well, Josie always says she isn't looking for a long engagement, for what it's worth."

Jaxon meets my gaze and mouths an "I'm sorry."

"It's true," Rosie pipes up from down the table. "She told me once she'd rather have the engagement and wedding in one fell swoop. Heck, didn't you say that you wondered why people even got engaged at all? That there's no point in waiting to start the rest of your life."

I look over at Josie whose cheeks are bright red. "Okay, new topic, please!" She laughs, but I can tell she's uncomfortable.

"Hey, it's okay to know what you want," I say, running my hand over her back. "I think that's pretty sweet. And you're right, Josie, if you know, why wait?"

I look over at Jonah who doesn't seem so convinced. His eyes are fixed on me with a scowl. And later, as everyone is cleaning up dinner, I see Josie drag him by the arm away from the crowd.

I try not to worry about what he is doing or saying to her or what she is saying to him.

I need to tell Josie the truth, so she can decide what man she really wants. I told the men I work for, but they agreed it is my story to tell.

But my time is running out, I can feel it. And I know I'm the man for her. I just need to make sure she knows that too.

CHAPTER SIX

Josie

*J*onah has been so ridiculous all week and tonight is no exception.

I pull him behind the garage, ready to give him a piece of my mind.

"What the heck, Jonah?" I'm angry at him for giving the man who is actually making me happy, such a hard time. "Why are you so intent on ruining this for me?"

Jonah frowns. "I'm not trying to ruin anything but Josie, what has Beau even told you about himself?"

"What do you mean? You think we don't talk? That we only have wild sex?"

Jonah raises his eyebrows. "I so don't need to hear that."

"Oh, so you're free to sleep around, but if I

have sex with someone you're gonna judge me? That's seriously so messed up, Jonah."

He runs his hands through his hair. "I know. I don't mean it like that. I just... Josie, I care about you. And the last thing I want is to see some guy none of us really know hurt you."

"You aren't my boyfriend, Jonah. You don't get to decide who I hang out with."

"I know." Jonah kicks the gravel, shoving his hands in his pocket. "I know I'm not your boyfriend, but I am your best friend. And I'd think you would at least consider what I'm saying."

My defenses are on high alert, and I don't know why except for the fact that I really like Beau and my best friend doesn't think we fit.

"Why don't you think he's the right guy for me anyway?"

"I just know how much you value honesty and I know for a fact he hasn't told you his whole story. And after hanging out for a week, having him come inside your house and all, I just think he should have by now."

"How do you know that? What aren't you saying?"

Jonah raises his hands and steps away. "It's something Hawk mentioned, about Beau's past. Look, I don't want to get in the middle of anything, but as your friend, I think you need to ask him where he's been the last five years."

"Fine," I say, crossing my arms. "I'll ask him. But we've been honest with one another, I know we have."

"Good. Then prove me wrong, Josie."

"Are you mad that you and I aren't ...."

Jonah shakes his head. "No, it isn't about being jealous. It's about wanting to make sure you're safe."

I snort. "This is about my safety now?"

"Josie, you can't seriously know someone in a week."

I tell Jonah goodbye, anxious to take Beau home and ask him more, wanting to believe that Jonah is wrong about everything.

And I do know that he's wrong about really knowing someone in a week.

Maybe I don't know everything about Beau Montgomery, but I know enough.

I know that I am falling for him.

--

In my room that night, I undress, slipping on a cotton nightgown and letting down my hair. Beau comes in the room, wrapping his arms

around me from behind, pulling me against him.
I let my head fall back against his chest, but
feeling as if there is something holding me back
from giving him more.

Jonah's words from earlier have been on my
mind for hours. After I spoke with him, I tried
to recover and focus on my friends and the
kiddos running around at the BBQ, but my
mind kept going back to what Jonah said. That
he knows Beau is holding something back.

"You okay, Jo?" Beau asks, pushing aside my
hair and kissing my ear.

"Yeah, it was a long night is all."

"Is that all it is?" He holds me tighter, and in
his arms, I do feel safe but I wouldn't be honest
with myself, or him, if I don't say something.

"I don't know. Jonah got in my head
tonight." I turn to face Beau, wanting to see his
eyes for this. "He seems to think you have
parts of your past you're avoiding telling me
about."

Beau's arms are around me, and I feel him
tense at my words.

"Is there something I should know?" I ask.

"I'm not trying to hide anything from you,
Josie, but Jonah isn't wrong." Beau exhales as if
whatever comes next takes his breath away.

I swallow hard, already feeling myself pull
back, wanting to wrap my heart in a protecting

layer, so it won't get broken during whatever conversation comes next.

"I've known you a week, Josie. And I don't want to scare you with the truth of my past."

"So, you've been doing more than build houses since you moved to Idaho?"

He nods, pulling away and walking toward the half-open window. The crescent moon is behind him, and the sliver of light seems to illuminate the reality of how little I know Beau. *Really know him.*

"Josie, I don't want to hurt you. And maybe it was wrong not to tell you straight away, but I didn't know that a week in, I'd feel like this."

"Feel like what?"

"Feel better when you're next to me. Feel complete when I can look over and see your face. Feel grounded when your body presses against mine. Dammit, Josie. I know it's been only a week and we haven't even had a proper date but you're making me crazy in a way that doesn't feel like chaos. It feels like you and I could build something together that is solid. That could stand the test of time."

His words peel away the protective layer. I feel it fall away and I fall more in love with him. There is no way I can protect my heart from Beau, because the truth is, it's like he already has it in his hands.

"You can tell me anything," I say. "Don't you trust me?"

He sits on the window ledge. "Of course, I trust you, but Josie, going to your friend's place tonight only emphasized how different we are. And I wonder if a man like me is going to ruin a girl like you. Maybe someone like Jonah is more deserv..."

I cut him off. I step toward him, pressing my hand to his lips, needing to contain those words that hold no ounce of truth.

"I don't want Jonah. And he doesn't want me. So, you can get that

out of your head for good."

"I want to believe you but he..."

"Stop it, Beau. Don't doubt me in this. Trust me. And let me trust you. Say whatever it is without being scared of me running away." I stand in front of him, between his knees. I won't let him talk me out of how I feel.

"I was in prison, Josie. For five years."

My eyes widen. I prepared myself for a lot of scenarios... an ex-wife, a child, debt ... but prison?

"For what?"

Beau's eyes meet mine. They are deep pools of blue and the sorrow they hold seems to spread the breadth of the ocean.

"For dealing drugs and trafficking guns."

My brows furrow. I can't reconcile the Beau I know with a man who sells drugs and guns. Not to the point of being sentenced to prison.

For five years.

But even still, I feel my body react to the words. I feel safe with him but should I?

"Who...? I mean, how?"

"I was driving a car filled with drugs. Not to mention a shit ton of cash and a trunk full of guns." His words force a chill over my bones. And for a second, I question all that I know about Beau. The room is still, and I want to erase the words he has said.

Then he speaks again and it changes everything.

"But the thing is, Josie. It wasn't me. I was framed."

"You didn't do it?" I shake my head. "You're saying you went to prison for five years for a crime you didn't commit?"

"Exactly. I ran around with some guys who used my trust against me. They screwed me over, and now... Shit. I'm fucking terrified I'm gonna lose you over it."

"But you don't just get framed. The evidence must have been..."

"It was bad. I'm telling you. I'm loyal to a fault. And when my friend Tommy realized that he planted me in a car, knowing it was either him that would be busted or me."

"Beau, why didn't the investigators believe you?"

"Tommy knew what he was doing. I was in the wrong place at the wrong time more than once."

"Have you seen him since you got out?" I know my voice trembles, but I don't know how to still it.

"No. But I heard that was looking for me. Has questions only I can answer. But I don't know anything about him. Not now and clearly, I never really did. That's why I left town the moment I got out. I wanted to start over."

He looks so broken like his story nearly breaks him and I want to be the woman who holds him up, helping piece him back together.

"This is why I didn't tell you," he says. "I went to prison, the things I've seen. Fuck, Josie. I know you say you trust me, but believing my innocence is something a judge couldn't even do."

I press my hands to Beau's cheeks. "I believe you."

His eyes search mine. "Why?"

"Because I choose to."

He shakes his head. "I've seen too much, Josie. You're nothing but innocence and beauty and a life I know nothing about. This whole town is too good for me. I don't deserve..."

"Stop it, Beau. Stop saying what you don't deserve. It's not how the world works. And fair isn't equal." I blink away my tears, so wanting to be the someone solid Beau needs. I want to be his rock and together I want to build a foundation.

And maybe it's crazy to want all that, so soon. Maybe my desire is blinding me from some truth but I don't care. Right now, I'm willing to risk it all.

I watched Buck and Rosie do that. So, did Harper and Jax and Hawk and Honor. This entire mountain was built on choosing to love when it seemed like the biggest risk of all.

"You've known me a week, Josie. You can't..."

"Stop it," I say, louder than I intended. My eyes lock on his. "Let me love you, Beau."

His eyes are filled with tears now. This rock-solid man, with a mountain man beard and a rugged truck and a wild heart, he is crying when he looks in my eyes. "You love me?"

"I think I do, Beau. I'm not looking for the perfect man. I am looking for a man who feels deeply and understands that life is precious. I want someone who isn't scared of things being hard. I want a man who will fight for love. Fight for me."

"Let me be that man for you, Josie."

"Even with all the risks? Without any guarantees?" I ask.

"Even with."

"Make love to me, Beau. Please," I beg. Needing his hands on my bare skin and wanting his heart to beat hard against my chest and longing for his arms to cradle me through the night.

We don't know everything there is to know about one another, but as he carries me to the bed, presses himself inside me, and kisses my lips with a tenderness I've never felt from a man before, I choose the risk.

Love rewards the brave, after all.

And right now, with Beau Montgomery, I choose to be brave.

I choose to trust in his innocence.

CHAPTER SEVEN

Beau

*A*s another few weeks pass, Josie and I fall into a rhythm. She works at the diner until mid-afternoon while I'm working on her house and then we spend the rest of the daylight hours memorizing one another's bodies. After we make love, we make dinner.

As she stirs spaghetti sauce, I make a salad. It feels good, after so long, to do something domestic. Even though I held a grudge against Judge Smith for a long time for putting me behind bars, right now, I realize all that has happened brought me to the here and now.

Cooking beside a beautiful woman, who has accepted me, despite my baggage.

"Too sweet?" Josie asks, holding a wooden spoon up to my mouth.

I taste the tomato sauce and shake my head.

"It's perfect, girl, just like you." I kiss, her, loving the way she looks in her apron, and it's impossible for me to keep my hands off her. She swats me away as I try to lift her shirt, her giggles filling the kitchen that's barely still in working order.

After supper, we work on the kitchen project together. Right now, we're peeling off the wallpaper; a steamer in her hand and a wall scraper in mine. Tedious, but she's adorable with a kerchief holding her hair back, biting her bottom lip as she moves the steamer up and down, slowly and methodically, making me smile the whole time. Even though sticky glue covers us and the remnants of the fifty-year-old paper attaches itself to our arms and legs as we work.

But damn, it feels good to do this together, and while I may have been with other women in my younger years, I never stood beside a woman demolishing a kitchen.

We are building this place back up, one job at a time. And it feels so damn good to be putting something together after five years of feeling like I was doing nothing but getting torn down.

While we work, she asks about prison and I appreciate her ability to face something head-long. This girl doesn't tiptoe. She makes a choice and sticks too it. At least as far as I can tell. And her ability to take my stories and accept them without judgment, draw me closer to her than I've ever been with another person in my life.

"Do you believe things happen for a reason?" she asks, on her knees as she steams the paper along the floorboards.

I think about how to answer as I move the scraper over the loosened paper and push it away.

"I guess, if I didn't it would mean you and I were nothing but coincidence."

"And you think we're more than that?" she asks.

"I think coincidences are for people without imagination," he says.

She laughs. "And you're Mr. Imagination? "

I press my lips together, cocking my brow. "What, you think I don't do anything out of the ordinary? Don't know how to use my imagination to get a little crazy? Have a little spontaneous fun?"

"Um. Not really," Josie says looking at me like I don't know a thing, her smile hidden by a smirk. "No offense, Beau, but no one would describe you as spontaneous."

"Guess I need to do something to change that," I say, picking her up and throwing her over my shoulder.

"Beau," she squeals in my arms, kicking playfully. "Put me down, you crazy man."

"Not a chance, sweet cheeks," I say, carrying her upstairs. She's a sticky mess, and I'm no better. In the bathroom, I set her down, turning on the shower and then picking her back up and setting her inside the claw foot tub.

"Are you nuts? I'm dressed!" she cries as the shower head sprays her down. "Beau!"

"Then you better get out of those clothes," I tell her, keeping the shower curtain open, and crossing my arms, watching as she hurriedly removes her clothing, shimmying out of her cut-offs and peeling her tank top over her head. In seconds, she's naked and the hot water runs in rivulets over her bare skin.

"What are you smiling about?" she asks. "You're getting in here too, mister."

"That tub won't fit us both," I tell her, eying the space. My broad shoulders and taller than average height were not meant to fit under that showerhead.

"Then let's take a bath," she says. She reaches for the tub stopper and the tub begins to fill. She adds bubble bath, then puts her hands on her hips. "Now get in here, Beau Montgomery, and clean me up."

I can't resist her, not when she's smiling like that. Her breasts so damn tempting and her round ass bare, but even when this girl is fully dressed, I know I'm hopeless for her.

As I step into the hot water in the quickly filling tub, I pull her down on top of me. The water splashes over the sides and I know we're making a mess, but neither of us cares. The bubbles surround her, and our laughter fills the hundred-year-old bathroom that hasn't seen this much action in decades, far as I can tell.

She sinks down on me, our bodies barely fitting, and we crack up as we awkwardly adjust. I pull her mouth to mine, kissing her hard, loving the way she opens against me, her pussy and my cock finding where they belong even if we're in a bathtub made for one.

"Is this enough imagination for you, Josie?" I ask. Her laughter turning to whimpers as she rides my hard cock.

"Yes. This is no coincidence. This is..." She stops talking then because an orgasm washes over her and she grips the edge of the tub as she comes so fucking hard.

But I don't need her to finish the sentence. I already know how it is supposed to end.

With her in my arms, forever.

This is no coincidence. This is love.

. . .

A few days later, we pull up to her father's house. It's a few hours from the mountain, but it was a gorgeous drive through a forest of pine trees. We arrive in Boise before dinner time, and within a few minutes, I wished I were back at her Granddad's house--back in the country--away from the traffic and Super Wal-Marts and fast food chains.

And that is just the half of it. The truth is, I'm not interested in running into anyone I used to know. Least of all Tommy. I haven't heard a word about him since I moved to the woods, but danger seems to be lurking around every corner in a major city and I don't want Josie to be in harm's way.

Tommy is not to be trusted.

But the dinner with her dad was inevitable. I know things are going fast with Josie and me, but I don't intend to put the brakes on anytime soon. She is the only woman I want.

Still, dinner with her dad makes me a little uneasy. The idea of sitting up straight with a man who I know works for the state makes me uncomfortable.

"And what exactly does your father do?" I'd asked her before, but she was always vague about his occupation.

"He's a judge, here in Boise."

"Like a legit judge?" I ask as the wheels of my truck grind to a halt.

She nods. "Are you mad I didn't tell you? Everyone always gets all nervous when they hear what he does for a living. Makes people think he's gonna be giving them the stink eye. That's why I didn't mention it."

"It's okay. I mean, he's gonna tell you I'm not good enough, but I can cross that bridge when we get to it."

I turn off the ignition, looking at her father's mansion. I know her mom died when she was little and that she's an only child, but I guess I didn't realize how loaded her father was. I swallow, wondering how he will size me up. The idea of proving myself to him seems impossible, but I'll try--hell I'll do whatever it takes to win him over.

"Don't assume the worst," Josie says, reaching for my hand. "Once he gets to know you he will see what a wonderful man you are. We can show him all the work on Granddad's house and he'll be impressed. I'm sure of it."

I nod, wanting to trust her.

Holding her hand, we walk to the door and she pushes it open without knocking. I suppose it makes sense. She grew up here, but as she calls for her dad, I'm forced to think about my own father. The deadbeat alcoholic who never changed, no matter how badly I needed a parent.

I know she holds her father in high regard and hell, he's a judge, so it's no wonder why.

I run a hand over my beard and follow her inside.

But then I see him.

Her dad.

And my vision goes blurry.

My memories return.

No. Fucking. Way.

CHAPTER EIGHT

Josie

I don't know what is happening, but it's bad. I look at my father and it's as if he's seen a ghost--but my dad doesn't believe in the supernatural--he only believes in what he can see with his own two eyes.

Facts and justice and honor and integrity. Those are the pillars that rule his life.

"What is it?" I ask, looking from him to the man beside me. The man who has shown me what it means to open my heart to love when I least expected to find it. The man who swept into my diner and sat down to eat and somehow filled the empty spaces of my heart within a few days.

But something is wrong. Beau's face is tense, his eyes narrow, anger rising in him and he takes a step back from my father.

"Beau, this is my dad, Judge Michael Smith."

"Smith." Beau looks at me. "I knew you were Josie Smith, but this... he can't...

Beau looks like he's seen a ghost too. Or maybe his scariest nightmare.

"What the hell is this man doing here, with you, Josie?" Dad asks with a steady voice that tells me something serious is happening. Dad has always been able to see through the bullshit and understand right from wrong. When his voice gets low and gravelly it is because he isn't messing around.

"What?" I ask, shaking my head in confusion. "Daddy, why are you getting so mad?" I wasn't expecting sunshine and rainbows from this first dinner together, but I also wasn't expecting such hostility. "This is Beau. Beau Montgomery. My boyfriend."

"Your what?" Dad nearly chokes as he asks the question.

"My boyfriend."

"I heard that," Dad says. "But this man is--"

Beau looks at me, the hurt in his eyes palpable. "Your father was the judge who sent me to prison, Josie. He is the man who--" Beau stops. And I can see by his clenched fists that he is ready to burst with rage. I've never seen him mad. Sad, sure, when he confessed to me the story of his past, but this emotion is something else entirely. This is fury.

"The man who determined that you should remain behind bars," my dad says vehemently. "I remember you, Beau Montgomery. How dare you try and--"

"He didn't do it, Dad," I say. "He's innocent." But even as I say it, I find myself second guessing my words.

How could my dad, the most respected man I know, who has spent his career determining right from wrong--be wrong now?

But then I look at Beau, his story having sounded so genuine, so honest... suddenly sounding foolish if I were to repeat it to my dad.

"This can't be happening, Josie. This bastard and you... He told you he was innocent? Even though the evidence pointed to this piece of work? You need to leave. You aren't welcome in my home. Not now, not ever."

I look at Beau, his eyes burning with anger as I reach for him, not wanting him to leave. But he flinches at my touch.

"I won't stay where I'm not wanted," he says.

"No, don't go, Beau. Dad." I look from one man to the other, my heart is torn and broken. They both can't be right, yet one of them is wrong.

I squeeze my eyes shut, completely unable

to comprehend a world in which neither of these men is in it. Knowing if my father is telling the truth, then that means Beau has been lying to me this entire time.

It would mean Beau is terrifying in the worst way.

"You are smarter than this, Josie," Dad says. "I remember this case clearly even though it was five years ago. You don't forget a name like Beau Montgomery and you certainly don't forget the images of a trunk filled with those kinds of weapons." My father shakes his head in disgust. "Selling drugs to kids. That's what this man you are with was doing."

I cover my mouth, unable to imagine Beau doing that.

"It's time you go."

"Daddy, don't..." I say, but even I know my words sound weak. Allowing Beau to stay means I'm telling my father, to his face, that I think he is a liar. That he gave a wrong judgment.

Beau turns to face me. He presses a hand to my cheek, not looking in my father's direction.

"Listen to me, Josie. I've been working on borrowed time my whole damn life. I should have prepared myself for losing you, but dammit, girl," he says, "I love you but looks like you've already made your choice. I'm outta here."

I falter at his words, scared. We haven't said *I love you...* not so explicitly and a sliver of doubt creeps into my mind. Is he only saying it now because he's scared of losing me?

By not answering though, it seems Beau has an answer.

He shakes his head. He lets go of my cheek, looking my father in the eyes. "You're wrong about me. You don't know where I come from and you don't know what I'm capable of. But that also doesn't mean you know what kind of man I am. It means you never will."

Beau leaves then, heading out the front door, leaving it open and getting in his Scout International. I walk to the front porch, my cheeks wet with tears and confusion wracking my body.

I made a mistake.

I made a mistake.

But then my dad wraps an arm around my shoulder and tells me it's all going to be okay.

I want to believe him.

But right now, I can't see anything clearly.

Right now, everything is a broken blur.

CHAPTER NINE

Josie

*G*rowing up with a father who is a judge meant that as a teenager, curfews were enforced. There was no gray area when it came to parties and if I wanted to date someone, they better pass Dad's personal background check.

But as I got older, Dad grew slightly more relaxed, realizing at some point that when I was in college he couldn't dictate whether or not I went to a kegger at a frat house.

It's been years since I brought a guy home, but even then, it was never a man like Beau. A man with muscles and true grit and eyes that told a story my father never lived, not by a long shot.

My dad always made six figures, had

colleagues who respected him, and the greatest heartache of his life was losing my mom. But even her death was something he prepared for. She had cancer and we all had time to say goodbye. Of course, there is never enough time when it comes to losing the love of your life, but he had decades' worth of memories with her and he always said he was lucky to have had the chance to love her at all.

But I should have been more thoughtful.

I'm so selfish. And as I watch Beau drive away in his truck, the realization hits me hard.

I should have been more thoughtful toward my father, and more thoughtful toward Beau. I was so caught up in my own love story I forgot that fact this would blindside them both.

Beau went to prison and my father sent him there.

"Josie," Dad says, calling me back inside. "Let's get you inside, sweetheart."

I let him wrap his protective arm around me, and then I ask to see the pictures from Beau's case. It's impossible to reconcile the man who I gave my heart to with the man my father called a monster.

"Josie, I don't think that's such a good idea. Why don't we eat? I made a roast chicken."

I shake my head. "I'm not hungry. It's just a lot to take in, Dad. I love Beau, but now? It's just more than I can take." I start crying in my hands, my shoulders shaking.

"Oh, Josie. Love? He's a criminal."

"I need to see to believe, Dad."

He must realize it's a lost cause to try and reason with me.

"Hold tight, Josie. Go get something to drink and I'll go look at some old files, okay? Maybe if you saw some pictures of what he was carrying in that car you'd understand."

I nod, wiping my eyes. "Thank you, Daddy."

"Anything for you, Josie. I just hate to see you cry."

He walks away, and I am grateful he is such a reasonable father. He's doing everything he can to make sure I'm okay, which makes my head and heart ache.

Beau lied to me.

Broke my heart.

A while later, Dad calls me into his study and asks me to take a seat in front of his computer monitor.

The images he shows me cause me to flinch, gasp, and shake my head.

No. No. No.

I want to believe Beau Montgomery, but the truth is that while Beau had the drugs and the guns and the money-- he had no alibi.

My father sent him to prison with a good conscience.

I thought I fell in love with Beau in the space of a few weeks, but maybe that isn't how love works. Maybe my friends just got lucky when they fell head over heels in a few days flat. Maybe my love story won't ever look like theirs.

Because I fell hard too and look what happened.

My heart cracked into a thousand pieces.

CHAPTER TEN

Beau

*M*y heart's a fucking tornado as I drive back to the mountain. I am a man filled with fury, a storming vessel that is hell-bent on destruction.

Right now, though, the only thing I want to ruin is myself.

I spent my life being in the wrong place at the wrong time and today is no fucking exception.

I told Josie my truth and it wasn't enough. I told her about prison and being wrongfully sentenced, but that isn't enough either.

The goddamn story of my life.

The man I am is never enough.

And damn, Josie is more than enough. She is my goddamn everything.

I want to get hammered. I want the memories of her father telling me to get off his property to fade into oblivion.

I pull my truck into the bar at the base of the mountain. This watering hole is nothing but a dive, and that is the perfect place to drown.

I push into the bar, and who do I see sitting at that bar but Hawk and Jax, a pitcher of beer between them. I lower my head, running a hand through my hair, not in a place to fucking tell a soul what just went down.

"Hey, Beau," they call out. "Take a seat, man."

I can't just turn and walk away, so I man up and head their way.

"What's up, man? Thought you were going to Josie's dad's tonight."

I shake my head and Hawk hands me a beer. "I was there, but I left pretty damn fast. It got ugly."

Jaxon narrows his brows. "What happened?"

I groan, fucking hating the truth of it. Still, I know Jax took a chance on me and I owe him this much.

I tell them the shitty truth, and when I finish, they're shaking their heads. "Look, I don't expect shit from you guys. You want me out, I'll go. But the truth is, I didn't lie to Josie. I know the man whose crime I paid for."

"Do you know where the guy is?" Hawk

asks. "Because the only way you're going to clear your name is if you find him."

Jax twists his lips, doubting that. "I don't know, man. What is Beau gonna do? Drag him by the neck to Josie's dad's house and force a confession?"

I sit up straighter. "That's exactly what I should do, but fuck, he won't go down without a fight. He has connections, you know?"

Hawk runs a hand over his beard. "When James was looking for Cherish, we drove all over the Pacific Northwest looking for her. You can't quit before you've even started."

"I can go looking for Tommy, but he is the sort of man who will only be seen when he wants to be found."

"He knows you're out?" Hawk asks.

I nod. "Apparently, he was looking for me. Wants to kill me before I can fucking make him pay. Which I don't even intend to do."

"Can you get him here?" Hawk asks.

"What do you mean?"

"I mean, let Tommy know you wanna talk. Lure him in. Then take him down."

The thought of fighting the kind of fight Tommy would be interested in makes me sick. I can't fucking do prison again.

But that was before Josie.

"How badly do you care about being with Josie," Jaxon asks. "Because if you don't..."

I cut him off. "It may have only been a few weeks, but that girl is my world. I'll fucking do anything to have her trust."

I don't want to fucking tear up in this bar, so I clench my fists under the table, trying to get myself in check. I came in here tonight looking to forget, but now...?

Now, all I want to do is remember.

Josie.

I will get her back, even if it's the last thing I do.

CHAPTER ELEVEN

Josie

*I*t can't be happening.

No.

No. No.

But it is.

Positive.

I'm on the pill but I guess in this case, statistics weren't on my side.

There is no doubt about it.

I took ten tests to be sure.

"Josie?" Dad calls, knocking on the bathroom door. "We really need to get to the college registrar's office before it closes. They're expecting us, so you can sign up for classes."

With shaky hands, I know I can't hide this. Nothing good will come of that.

Especially after my Dad has been nothing but patient with me the last few weeks. He's talked through options with me. We've made lists of pros and cons.

Options:

1) Stay at Granddad's house and work at the diner.

2) Move back to the city and work on my master's degree.

I know I don't want a job at a bank, I'd want a master's degree in finance that could help families make choices to give them financial freedom. At least it would be a job I'd feel good about.

But these options offer drastically different lives.

And I love the mountain. I do. And Granddad's house feels like home, but Beau is there.

And I don't want to let one man determine my life choices, but at the same time, staying there, hoping for a new man to waltz into town and give me the life I want seems so ridiculous. Instead, I could have a career and make my own life without waiting for a man to give it to me.

I know what Dad thinks.

But those lists were made before I took these tests today.

"Dad," I say, putting on my bravest face and opening the bathroom door. "I have to tell you something."

"What is it?" he asks, his eyes wide with concern as he takes in my blotchy face.

"I'm pregnant. With Beau Montgomery's baby."

"When are you coming back?" Jonah asks. I've been at my dad's for over a month. At first, I planned on going back to the mountain but now everything has changed.

But I don't know how to tell my best friend that.

My dad took it well as if he had prepared himself for the worst. Maybe after a lifetime of working with criminals he had.

But being pregnant is not a crime.

It's a gift, a blessing... at least in a lot of cases.

And even though my child is the size of a blueberry, it feels like a burden too heavy for me to bear.

"I don't know when I'll be back," I say honestly. "I think I'll be here awhile though. Knowing Beau's still at the mountain, it's hard to imagine returning."

"So, you're just staying away for good

because he lied?"

"I don't know. I love him, Jonah. Or at least loved him. I don't know." I brush away the tears and am grateful I didn't place this call on FaceTime.

"I know, Josie. But everyone here feels like they're between a rock and a hard place. The men on this mountain are all about second chances and Beau's a hard worker who's helping Buck and Jaxon out. And you know how Hawk influences their opinions. He's all about letting Beau stay--especially since he served his time. People change, you know?"

"But he still lied to me, Jonah. And I'd be lying if I said this didn't hurt.

My closest friends are siding with him."

"No one's siding with anyone, Jos." Jonah sighs, and I hate that I'm putting him in the position to be the go-between. It isn't fair. "Maybe it's best for you to stay at your dad's place until you start to feel less..."

"Heartbroken?"

"Yeah."

I swallow; the whole truth on the tip of my tongue, but I'm scared Jonah will accidentally say more than he should to my friends out on the mountain.

"Okay, enough about me," I say to avoid

talking anymore about myself. "How are things on your end?"

Jonah sighs through the phone. "Steph says she's gonna come visit this summer. You think that's a bad idea?"

I sit cross-legged on the carpet in my bedroom and think about that for a second. Steph was his girlfriend last year when he was living in Florida. She worked at a tattoo parlor and though I've never met her, I know she and Jonah fought a lot.

And then she cheated on him.

"I don't know. I mean... Do you think she wants to get back together?" I ask gently.

"It's hard to be on this mountain and not have anyone."

He doesn't have to tell me that. It's the exact reason I don't want to return. The idea of being back there, with all the sugary romance and adorable babies and seeing Beau? My heart turns to knots just thinking about it.

Besides, I am not ready to tell him I am carrying his baby.

"What about Grace?" I ask. "Could you and she be something?"

Grace had been held hostage at the same cult as Cherish, plus she and Jonah have similar childhoods.

"There's nothing there, Josie." Jonah laughs. "Believe me, I tried, just like I tried with you."

"You never know when you're going to meet your person, Jonah, but going back to a girl who hurt you doesn't seem like a step in the right direction and I think you know that."

"It gets old, though, not having someone." Jonah exhales and the sadness in his voice is hard to miss. "I just want to start my life with someone you know?"

"I know." My voice hitches and tears spring to my eyes. I squeeze them shut, thinking only about Beau.

Thinking *always* about Beau.

The way he ran his fingers over my bare skin, pulling back the layers of my heart and the way he planted something fierce in my heart. Love blossomed in that space... and then, then it's as if someone yanked that seedling and stomped on it. I thought it our love was strong but turns out it was fragile.

And now?

Now it is nothing but a withered vine, and something dead can never grow.

I'm not ready to watch it die, though. My tears water that fading plant, unable to let go.

I want it to grow.

I want something that will never be.

"Josie," Jonah says more softy. "I'm sorry for

what Beau did to you, but you're gonna be okay. You're a survivor."

I laugh bitterly. "Says the guy who literally survived living in a cult for twenty years."

"It's okay to feel betrayed, but this feeling won't last forever. I promise. And when you're ready to come back home, you have a lot of friends waiting with open arms."

We hang up and the knot in my heart twists even more.

Even with everything I know, I miss Beau.

CHAPTER TWELVE

Beau

For the next month, I work for Jax's crew during the week, saving money to spend it on fixing up Josie's house. I'm not gonna paint and redecorate, I know women like to pick out that stuff, but I do know how to replace the electrical, install new lighting, and fix worn floorboards. She had a lot of stuff already picked out for her kitchen and I still have the keys to her house.

She told Jax to pause on the project until she knew what she wanted to do with the property. I guess her dad talked her into considering selling it. But I figure even if she sells, she'll get more from the sale if it's updated.

But I'm hoping once I find a way to clear my name, she will see as the man I am.

Hers.

I rebuild that house from the ground up.

Jaxon knows what I'm up to, but he has chosen to turn a blind eye. Something about knowing that working for a woman's heart takes time. He told me it took him and Harper a long time to find common ground, but once they found their footing, they had a foundation that would last a lifetime.

I want that too.

With Josie.

Only Josie.

So, after I work on the crew's job site, I put in my evening hours at Josie's place. With one nail at a time, I'm putting her place back together.

It's all I can do until I find Tommy.

On the weekend, I hop in my Scout and try to find my way back to the beginning.

Already knowing how I want my story to end.

With Josie.

Only Josie.

Always Josie.

Another month passes, and I'm sitting on Josie's

front porch on a self-imposed break, drinking a glass of water at nearly ten o'clock at night, when headlights roll down the driveway. Jonah steps out of the truck and when he steps out, heads my way, I know he was out looking for me.

"Josie know you're out here?" he asks, walking up to me, giving me a long look.

I shake my head. "Nah. But we talked about what she wanted. I'm not doing anything cosmetic, just rewiring, patching old drywall, that kinda shit."

Jonah nods, extra slowly, and I don't know where he stands.

"You talk to her?" I ask, wanting to know every last detail.

"I have. A few times. But she, uh..." He stops, runs a hand over the back of his neck and sits down on the step next to me. Usually, at job sites, he's stiff and withdrawn around me, like he's dead set against getting to know me. "But uh, she sounds off, man."

"Off, like how?"

Jonah looks at me, the porch lamp casting a light bright enough that I can see him. He looks pained.

"Off like sad. I asked if I can go visit if she wants to come out, but all I get is no. Over and over. It isn't like her. She's saying the same thing to the girls, Rosie and Harper have tried. It's like she's a different person, totally withdrawn."

"You think it's her dad pressuring her to get away from here?"

"It's what I'd guess."

I run a hand over my beard, not at all sure of why Jonah came to me, to tell me this.

"What are you getting at, Jonah?"

He exhales, like this conversation fucking pains him.

"Look, I don't know what your deal is, okay?" he says coolly. "I know the other guys trust you, but I don't take their side. I take Josie's. And she's a mess."

"You're her best friend, aren't you? Why don't you help her?"

"That's the thing, man; she doesn't want my help." He looks me dead on. "She is fucking in love with you. And I don't know a lot about love but I do know that whatever happened between the two of you, it was more than she's letting on. She needs a man. Her man. And that man's not me. It's you."

"It's not that easy. I can't find the man who wronged me. Until I do..."

"Let me help. I fucking helped James scour the northwest. I'm actually pretty damn good at it."

"You want to help me?"

"I want to help you help Josie."

"You sure you don't love her?"

Jonah tells his jaw, his mouth in a firm line. "I love her like a sister. When I moved here we just kinda fit together, not in an intimate way. In a breath of fresh air way. We became friends, and that's why I want to help you. Besides," he laughs. "Who else is gonna help you? The rest of this mountain is covered in babies. No one else has time to chase down this asshole who should be in prison."

"Thank God you're still single then, Jonah, because I could really use a hand."

Jonah and I sit out there, on the porch. I grab us some beers and we sit and shoot the shit--and I realize why Josie got along with him so well. He's a straight shooter and yet he isn't all uptight. He's solid, been through a fuck ton of shit. At least we have that common ground.

I don't know what is going on with Josie, or why she's pushing everyone away--but I'm gonna do all I can to fix what I've broken.

For Josie.

For us.

CHAPTER THIRTEEN

Beau

*I*t's been over three months since I've seen Josie.

Since I heard her voice.

And no one is getting much from her, except the girls say she'll FaceTime every few weeks--so at least they know she is well.

But I am a man on a mission.

I will win my woman back.

When Jonah and I leave Stan's place, I have a bad feeling that shit is gonna go down really fucking fast.

"I don't want shit to come to the mountain," I tell Jonah as we drive back. "But unless Tommy comes out of the woodwork I have no choice."

Stan told us he would talk about around the neighborhood, with the hope being that he dropped enough hints Tommy's guys would know where to come looking.

"Stan seems a little over his head," Jonah says as I head toward the highway.

"I know," I say, gripping the wheel. "And I don't want something to happen to him. He's an old man and doesn't need to deal with Tommy or his thugs." I shake my head. "Maybe it was a bad call, coming out to Stan like this; involving him."

"He wanted to help though," Jonah says. It's true, the moment I told Stan I wanted to be out, he agreed it was the only way I would ever relax. Otherwise, I'd spend my life looking over my shoulder to see if Tommy was out for me.

As we drive out of town, I think about Josie, Her dad's place is only ten minutes from here.

"Maybe we should stop at Josie's," I say, without really thinking it through.

"You want to?"

"Of course, I do," I say, scowling at Jonah. I turn on my blinker, turning toward her father's development.

When we get closer though, I start to doubt my plan. I want to see her, but I don't want to upset her.

Still, I can't help it.

When I pull up, there is a BMW in the

driveway and I try not to roll my eyes. I knock on the door, Jonah by my side, and wait.

Of course, it's her father, Michael, who answers.

"Is Josie here?" I ask.

Michael sneers. "I wouldn't tell you if she was."

"Hey," I say. "She's an adult. You can't keep that kind of thing from her. I need her to know that--"

"She doesn't need to know anything from you. But you need to go before I call the cops."

Jonah speaks up then, "Look, sir, I'm Jonah, her friend. Can you at least tell her--"?

"I won't at least anything. I know all about you Jonah. You're a backwoods kid who never graduated high school, and Josie is a--"

"Hey," I say, my voice rising. "Don't talk about Jonah like that, you hear me?"

"Oh yeah?" Michael crosses his arms, a smug look of satisfaction on his face. "Or what?"

I shake my head, knowing the only thing I can do is drop it. "You're wrong about me and about Jonah."

"Doesn't matter what I think, does it?"

I clench my fists, longing to fight, but instead, I step away, knowing the only way out of this is to find Tommy.

"This isn't over," I tell him. I head toward

my truck with Jonah, and as I jump in the driver's seat, I swear I see a curtain fall, and a person move.

I know Josie is in there. I know she heard me.

And for whatever reason, she's hiding something.

But I'm not.

For her, I'll put it all on the line.

CHAPTER FOURTEEN

Josie

I stand in my bedroom window, my hand resting on my baby bump, watching as Jonah and Beau drive away.

Tears fill my eyes as the reality washed over me.

When I didn't see Beau, it was easier to push down the memories of when I was with him, but then seeing him here, in the flesh, it's impossible to suppress what I know is real.

I love him.

I am in love with a criminal.

I am in love with a man my father calls a liar.

But part of me doubts that. I want to believe Beau with all that I am.

Maybe that makes me a monster.

Maybe that makes me insane.

But I don't care.

Not right now.

Right now, I just want Beau to hold me tight.

I press my hand to my belly, thinking about the baby I've started calling Blueberry, and try not to let myself get swallowed up in tears.

I can do this.

After Dad goes to bed I pack a bag. I'm going back to Granddad's.

I don't know for how long. Maybe a night. Maybe forever.

But I can't tell Dad, or he will give me a thousand reasons to doubt myself.

But something this good can't be wrong.

And Beau Montgomery and I are something so very good.

I get in my car, drive to the mountain, knowing that this is a bad idea on so many accounts.

Maybe it is reckless to leave like this, but this is the only way.

The stars are out, and the roads are clear, and the stereo blares my playlist, the one I made after Beau and I... well, after we met. The song *Home* is on repeat ...

Let me come home.

Home is whenever I'm with you.

When I pull up to Granddad's house, I see

I'm not the only one here. My eyes narrow as I realize the cars here aren't ones I recognize.

I reach for my phone, thinking maybe this is a bad idea. But before I can make a call, the driver's door swings open, and I am pulled from the car.

At gunpoint.

All I can think about is the baby I am carrying. How I never told Beau he is a father. How I should never have left like I did tonight, without telling a soul.

"What do we have here, a pretty little girl lost at night?" the man snarls. His breath is foul, his eyes beady under the headlights, and I want to fight him away, but he has me held tightly.

"Let me go," I scream, trying to kick him away, but then he has my feet, and wrestling away will only cause me to fall.

And I can't do anything that might harm the baby.

The gun gleams under the moon and the silver casing frightens me.

This can't be how my story ends.

Then my hands are bound with ropes, and I'm dragged into my house.

They push me inside; my eyes fill with tears as I see all the work that been done here. The kitchen is beautiful. The big white apron sink I dreamt about is mounted under a butcher-block countertop, open shelving and bright white tile and a vintage refrigerator in mint green.

I know Beau did this.

For me.

And I can't thank him. Because instead, I'm hit upside the head with a gun, and I fall to the ground, blacking out.

My eyes close and my last thought is, I should have believed him.

CHAPTER FIFTEEN

Beau

I've just gotten back to the trailer, thinking about going to sleep, but something in my gut tells me it's not the time to go to bed. It's the memory of that damn curtain falling, back at Josie's dad's house that has me making a pot of coffee at eleven p.m., knowing that I need to go to her Granddad's place and put in some hours fixing the drywall in the master bedroom.

I can't sit here in this trailer doing nothing. At least working at her house will feel like I'm accomplishing something in the name of love.

I grab my keys and just as I'm about to drive over, I get a call from Jonah.

"Hey man, I'm headed to the bar with Jax. Wanna come?"

"Thanks, but I'm gonna go fix up some drywall."

"Sure, man?" Jonah asks.

"Yeah, I gotta do something with my hands, man."

"Alright, man. Take it easy."

I end the call and pull out in my Scout. I get to her place in a few minutes, and as I pull up I realize right away something isn't right. My chest tightens--Josie's car is here. And she isn't alone.

Her car door, though, is left open, and I check the seat, seeing her phone and purse lying there. That's not like her. Without pause, I run toward the house, knowing something isn't right. I hurl myself up the porch steps and push through the front door.

That's when I see him.

Tommy. The man who fucking betrayed me.

"Look who we have here," Tommy sneers. "The man we were looking for."

I pull back my shoulders, not wanting to fight, but knowing that whatever comes next, I can't let them do something to Josie.

"Where is she?" I growl.

"Oh, is that your girl?" Tommy snorts. "I heard you were looking for me."

I step forward, knowing that even though Tommy is a monster of a man, I can take him down. I'm not just fighting for myself. I have Josie to fight for.

"I'm asking you nicely, one more time, then I am going to fucking make you tell me. Where is Josie?"

Tommy reaches into his pocket for a Glock, and I tense, knowing I am in trouble so fucking deep. I'm in a place I never wanted to go. Not now, not ever. Hell, I met these guys in a construction crew, when I was barely twenty fucking years old. I didn't know how shady they were. Only that they were in construction until they could make their way up in the black market.

I thought they were hard working guys, just like me; but instead, they are criminals.

Only I'm the one who paid for their fucking crimes.

I push forward, and Tommy raises his gun.

"Just tell me," I shout. Then I hear her. A muffled scream from the bedroom down the hall.

"You like it when your girl whimpers for you? Because if you don't tell me what I want to know, I will fucking make her beg."

"Don't talk about her like that," I hiss.

"Or what?" Tommy asks. He raises the gun and shoots. A bullet crashes through the front window, glass cascading to the floor. I want to kill him for ruining what isn't his to break. But before I can reach for him, I see movement in the corner of my eye from the kitchen.

It's Jax and Jonah, standing silently, a six-pack of beer in hand. Those guys are too fucking good--coming here with a beer to cheer me up.

And look at the danger I've brought them.

Brought everyone.

Josie.

I clench my jaw and shake my head, nearly imperceptibly, knowing I need to distract Tommy.

"I was looking for you," I tell him. "I heard you wanted some answers."

"I do. But I need to make sure you won't talk before I start asking."

"Won't talk about what?" I ask, stepping closer to him, not wanting to think I'm intimidated in the least.

Because I'm not. I went to prison. I can fucking handle a pussy like Tommy.

And I need to get this motherfucker to talk. I have the witnesses I need.

"Talk about the time you served."

"You mean the time I served for you, Tommy?"

Tommy shrugs. "You know we never meant to hurt you."

"Hurt me how? Because so far as I can tell, you are the one who planted that shit on me. Framed me."

"That's all water under the bridge now, Beau. Now I just want a chance to say good-bye."

"Goodbye, huh? That ain't happening."

At this Tommy's eyes narrow, and he steps toward me, placing his hand on the collar of my shirt. "I'm here for one reason. To make sure you never talk shit about me."

I shake my head. "You think I'd waste my breath on you?"

Tommy juts his chin to indicate his crew. "I got your girl, and I'm taking her with me."

With his gun raised, he drags Josie out to the front room. There's an open wound on her head, blood smeared across her forehead. I'll kill Tommy for doing this to her.

Her eyelids flutter open, and when she sees me, she gasps. "Beau?"

I nod, moving toward her, needing to cradle her in my arms and never let her go.

"What the fuck are you doing?" Tommy asks. "You don't get her unless you tell us where the money is. you piece of shit."

I clench my jaw, needing to get them away from Josie.

"You tried to send me to prison, Beau, and for that, you must pay."

I remember the night all too well.

It was pitch dark, and I was on the edge of town. Thought I was going to pick up Tommy's friend for him in a car Tommy had given me a month before. Convenient move on his part.

I was driving their shit, never realizing they were using me as cover in case they were caught.

By the time I realized what was happening, I knew running wouldn't work. I had opened the truck and saw the goods, and my fingerprints were on everything.

I was stuck there and paid for his crime--but that won't happen again.

Because as the cops blaze down the driveway toward the house, I thank God, Jax and Jonah showed up and had my back.

And Tommy, he's probably wanted on a dozen accounts. I can see it in his eyes.

"What the hell?" he yells, looking around, and seeing Jax and Jonah here. Jax moves behind him, and I reach for his gun, disarming him before he has a chance to do something even more stupid than hurt the woman I love.

Tommy tries to break free from Jax's hold, and Jonah is helping to hold him down.

"I have what I wanted, Tommy. Freedom. And I will never, ever, let you take it from me again."

The cops break through the door, guns

raised, and I drop to the floor. Not in surrender. I have nothing to hide.

I'm on my knees, scooping up the woman I love, and pulling her close.

I will never let her go.

CHAPTER SIXTEEN

Josie

*T*he police are here all night, taking our reports and taking into evidence Jonah's phone that contains the recording of Tommy's confession, clearing Beau's name once and for all. I'm so grateful Jonah pressed record and managed to get all of Tommy's incriminating words.

A doctor is here, and she's with me for a long time in a back bedroom to check if I am concussed. When I tell her I'm with child, her brows knit with worry. I explain the situation, and she leaves, only to return an hour later with a portable ultrasound machine.

I'm not sure why she felt so inclined to confirm that all was well with the baby, but she must have understood how badly I needed the confirmation that my baby is okay.

It is.

And I am anxious for everyone to leave so I can finally tell Beau. I've never wanted to tell someone anything so badly in my life. I almost died and he nearly did too, but we are alive, and we have a second chance.

When everyone finally leaves, and I finish talking to my dad on the phone then turn to see the house is finally empty.

"What did he have to say?" Beau asks, pushing back a strand of hair and pressing the ice pack to my wound. We're in the kitchen. The beautiful kitchen he's renovated, built for me with his blood, sweat, and tears. I sit on the counter, with him right in front of me.

"He feels awful. And embarrassed. And really, really sorry." My Dad's voice cracked when we spoke. When he heard all that went down tonight. For a second, I felt bad for him, for his wounded pride. Then I look over at Beau, his face written in worry, a man who had served so much time for something he never did and that I didn't even trust him.

I'm the one who should be most ashamed.

"But not as sorry as I am, Beau," I say, the tears falling down my cheeks. "I doubted you when you gave me no reason to."

"Shhh," he says. "It doesn't matter now. Now,

you're safe. And it's just you and me now. No one else will come between us."

That is when I start sobbing. The heaving in my heart must terrify him because he wraps his arms around me, and with my knees spread, he nestles between them, holding me so tightly.

"What is it?" he whispers as my tears fall on his shirt.

"It's not just us."

He cups my face in his hands, looking deep in my eyes. "What do you mean?"

I take his hand and rest it on my belly. "I'm pregnant, Beau."

It takes his breath away; this news. His face breaks into a smile so sweet that my heart melts.

"A baby?" he asks, shaking his head, tears in his baby blue eyes.

"I call it our little blueberry. I found out after I got to my dad's. I should have told you, but I didn't..." My lips tremble and I hate that I have kept this from him.

"It doesn't matter now. Thank God, you're both safe." Then his face creases with concern. "The baby is okay, right?"

I nod. "The doctor made sure of it. I was terrified we may have lost it, but we didn't, Beau."

His shoulders relax as he pulls me to him, and as his lips find mine any doubt I may have harbored about his desire to be a father vanishes. He wants this as much as I do. I can feel it as his hands run over my back, under my shirt, feeling my bare skin. His hands are warm and when he touches me, I feel his desire to protect me pressing softly against me.

He won't let me go.

"You are going to be such a good mother," he whispers, tilting my head back and kissing me again, our mouths parting as his words send a rush of pride through my body. His belief in my ability is more than I ever thought I would find. A real man who knows what truly matters in life.

I pull away from him, so I can see him more clearly, my body is hot and craving the man I have missed for so many weeks. "And you are going to be such a good Papa."

"Papa huh?" he asks.

"Mmmhhmm, it fits you."

"Oh girl, this is more than I ever thought I'd have."

"And what's that?" I ask, wanting him to spell it out again because the words make my heart burst with pleasure.

"A woman and a baby, in a house we built together."

"I haven't done much of the building," I tell

him. "Looks like you've been here every day. It's beautiful, Beau."

"Don't worry," he says, lifting up my tee-shirt, and throwing it to the side. "I'll put you to work."

He unclasps my bra, and then cups my breasts in his hands, kissing them tenderly, with devotion, before scooping me off the counter and tugging down my pants. He places my bare ass on the butcher block and I reach for the buckle of his jeans.

"I miss you, Beau, so much," I whimper, knowing his magnificent cock is within reach. "I want you so bad."

"Good, because I want you too," he says, dropping his boxers as my hands wrap around his length. His tip is so smooth, and his shaft is so hard and everything about his body is perfection--made for me.

"I love you, Beau Montgomery," I moan, my arms wrapping around his neck and he pulls me closer, pressing his hard cock against me.

"And I love you, Josie," he says, filling me up with all he has to give.

I cry out in pleasure as he moves against me, a hand on my ass, drawing me nearer to himself. He thrusts against me, and I stare at his rock-hard chest, the way his muscles move as he fills me up. I lose myself as we make love, on the counter, in this kitchen he built for me.

My body is on fire as his hard ridges move against my pussy, I'm so slick and ready for him and all I want is this to last forever.

Of course, it won't; but this life together can. And when I come against him, the orgasm rushing through me, blood pumping as his release fills me, I know this life together will. Will last forever.

"I love you," I whisper, squeezing my arms around his neck, clinging to him as if he is the life force I need to survive. And maybe he is. In this moment, he completes me.

He presses his hand to my belly. "Our little blueberry."

He lifts me from the counter, kissing me hard, taking my breath away and forcing my heart to explode. He is mine and I am his.

"Now," he says, kissing my neck, my ear, my nose. "How about we get a second serving of the Josie Special?"

He carries me to the bedroom, and we crash into the bed, falling deeper in love.

EPILOGUE 1

Josie: One Month Later...

There is only one question on the mountain after the dust settles from the criminal run-in at Granddad's house.

When is Beau Montgomery going to propose?

For a few weeks, I wonder if he even realizes I'm pretty much waiting on pins and needles for him to pop the question, but even after Harper nudges Jaxon to nudge Beau, there is no engagement.

I'm about to lose my mind and that's not just the crazy-making hormones of pregnancy talking.

I want a ring on my finger before this belly pops.

The diner has been slow all morning, yet Rosie keeps talking to the cook about putting more pies in the oven. I ask if there is a catering order I didn't know about, which she says there is.

But I can't think about catering and boxing up pies right now, my mind is occupied.

"You're being a little intense," Rosie says as we clear a table at the diner. With plates piled in my arms, I shrug, walking away from her. "You've only been back in town for a few weeks. Let him get adjusted to being a father before you start demanding a proposal."

"Easy for you to say, you already have what you want."

Rosie smiles. "Sure, but remember my road to getting there? I had to escape a freaking mafia ring to end up here."

"True. I'm an idiot." I press a hand to my forehead. "You're right. I already have everything that matters."

Rosie pats my back. "Relax and trust that everything will work out perfectly." Then she winks as the bells on the front door the dinner jingle, announcing another guest.

I turn around and see Beau walking in.

He gives me a sly smile as a grin spreads across my face. I reach for the coffee pot.

As I walk toward him, the whole gang pulls into the parking lot.

I turn back to Rosie. "What's everyone doing here?"

She just shrugs and heads to the backroom.

"What's going on?" I ask Beau as Harper, Cherish, Honor, Stella, and Grace come into the cafe with kids on their hips and holding the hands of little ones. I see the guys helping kids from carseats, and Beau just keeps his eyes on me--but he doesn't come over.

Then a U-Haul truck comes in the parking lot, reversing toward the back entrance.

Beau mouths the words, "I love you" and I mouth them back, but instead of coming over to me he is swept into the back of the kitchen with a few of the guys. Jonah follows them, giving me a thumb's up before he walks away.

"Everyone looks so nice," I say, catching Harper's eye. She just smiles, and tugs down the dress her daughter wears. My friends are all dressed to the nines-- which is saying something for a bunch of mountain men. And the women are in pretty dresses and their hair is done. Even the kids are all clean-faced with combed hair.

When my dad pulls into the parking lot I'm really confused. When he opens his trunk, and takes out bouquets of sunflowers I'm flabbergasted.

Behind me, Rosie says I need to follow her. "What is going on?"

"Relax, remember?"

I shake my head thoroughly confused, but then she drags me into her tiny office in the back of the diner and shuts the door.

"Okay, spill," I tell her.

"We don't have time for chit-chat, darling. You need to get dressed."

Just then Grace comes in with a garment bag. "I finished it in time. I swear my fingers were gonna bleed from the stitching--but it's done." She hangs the bag on the back door and pulls down the zipper revealing a beautiful, white gown.

"Oh, my gosh," I say, pressing my hands to mouth. "What is this for."

"It's your wedding day, Josie," Rosie tells me. "And it's time for you to put on your wedding dress."

"I hope you like it," Grace says. "You always said you didn't want a wedding with a lot of fuss, and it looks like your groom knows you well."

I let out a loud laugh, complexity shocked. "This is insane," I say, looking at the gorgeous dress. Simple, but with delicate lace on the neckline and sleeves. "I can't believe you made this, Grace."

She smiles. "Growing up in a cult taught me a few skills that are handy. I can sew and can, like nobody's business."

"And this is happening, like, now?"

Rosie nods. "Like right now."

In the diner, I hear the lyrics of my favorite song...*Home is when I'm alone with you.*

This is really happening.

My hands are shaking, my heart pounding.

"I don't think I can get dressed," I say laughing despite the insanity of what is happening.

"Let us help," Grace says. And so they do.

When I walk out of the office and head toward the diner, I see the place has been transformed in a matter of minutes. The tables are pushed against the walls, flowers are arranged on each of them. The kids and their parents all stand quietly, in a semi-circle. Music plays and Rosie hands me a bouquet, but all that fades away the moment I see Beau.

Beau wears a suit and his hair is pushed back from his eyes and he is nothing but a true mountain man, polished for his wedding day.

I only have eyes for him.

My father takes my arm, smiling at me in a way I never expected.

"Hey," I say softly. "You knew about this, Dad?"

"I did." My father looks at me with tears his eyes. "Beau came to my house two weeks ago and asked for my daughter's hand in marriage."

"And you said yes?"

"I said my daughter was a lucky woman."

Holding the sunflowers in one hand and my father's arm with the other, we walk down the makeshift aisle.

When I look at Beau, standing there, waiting for me, my heart skips a beat and I swear I'm going to trip. But then his eyes fix on mine again, and the world melts away.

Jaxon is the officiant, holding a paper with a script, I'm guessing, and he motions for me to stand opposite Beau as my father gives me away.

Beau smiles, shaking his head. "You're the most beautiful thing I've ever seen, Josie."

I press my lips together, knowing if the tears start they'll never stop.

"This is too much," I say, not understanding how I ended up with the life I always wanted. My friends and father are gathered around me, and I'm about to exchange vows at the very place I met the father of my child.

"Not too much," Beau says. "We will build this life together, and it will be everything we dreamed of, and more."

EPILOGUE 2

Beau: Two Years Later

My son, Forrest, bolts from the front door, and finds me on the front porch. His face turns into a toothy toddler grin and I reach for him, pulling him to my lap.

"Hey there mister, where do you think you're going?"

"Treat, Papa?" he asks with wide eyes, blue ones, matching my own. To say I'm a softie for this kiddo is an understatement. He came into our lives and opened our hearts. We thought we understood love before, but then we met Forrest and changed forever.

"Did your mama tell you to come ask me that?"

Josie hollers from the kitchen. "I said no such thing!"

Forrest erupts in giggles, then whispers, "Mama's muffins."

I furrow my brows. Then I sniff the air and nod. "You're right. Mama made cookies. What for?"

"The baby."

"Baby? We don't have a baby here," I say, tickling him. "You're a big boy."

I'm still amazed that my life consists of sitting on the front porch of my house, with my son in my arms. I don't know how I got it so damn good--but I swear, I'll never take it for granted.

"Mama baby," Forrest says, his little face scrunched up in question.

Before I can say anymore, Josie walks out of the house, a plate of muffins in hand. "Hungry, boys?"

"See, Papa!"

"I do," I say, ruffling his hair. Josie sits beside us, a smile on her face. "You're in a good mood," I say taking a muffin from the plate.

Why wouldn't I be?" She asks. "They're blueberry muffins."

"I see that. They look good."

"Why do you love blueberries so much, Mama?" Forrest asks.

I look down at my muffin, remembering the

way Josie always called Forrest our little blueberry.

My eyes meet Josie's, the love of my life, the woman I am so damn lucky to call my wife.

She bites her bottom lip. "Can you make a guess?"

I cock my head at her, nearly choking on the muffin as it dawns on me.

"We're having another baby?"

Her face is as bright as the first day we met when she reminded me of a sunflower in bloom.

"Twins!"

I wrap my arms around her, inhaling her lavender perfume that reminds me of when we first met. Forrest squeals as he's caught in between us, knowing he's safe and secure in our arms.

I kiss Josie, knowing that while our home is built on solid ground, our love is fucking indestructible.

Next in the the Mountain Man's Babies Series:
CHISELED

PLAYLIST FOR BUILT

♥**Josie's Favorite Song**♥:
**Home —Edward Sharpe & The Magnetic
Zeros**
And more inspiration for the story...
To Build A Home — The Cinematic Orchestra
All Is Well — Austin Basham
Mess Is Mine — Vance Joy
Rivers and Roads — The Head and the Heart
Shine — Sufjan Stevens
Higher Love — James Vincent Marrow
The Night We Met — Lord Huron
Build Me Up From My Bones — Sarah Jarosz

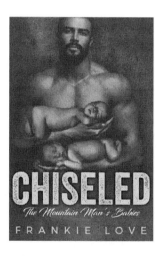

It's time to return to our favorite mountain—
where potlucks are plentiful, men know how to
change diapers, and there's a place for everyone
at the table. Grab a plate, scoop up some of
Harper's potato salad, get one of the burgers

Jaxon is grilling, and enjoy the peace and quiet while it lasts—goodness knows there are enough kids running around that you've gotta take it when you can!

The woods are heating up with CHISELED! It's Grace's turn to find her happily-ever-after ... but she's fallen for the reclusive mountain man named Bear! When a shocking package arrives at the doorstep of her cottage, she knows her world has just turned upside down— X 2!

#TheBeardGangIsBack #BabiesForDays #IsThisRealLifeEven #TheFertileMountian #iLostCount #MeToo #TooMuch #NeverTooMuch #GimmeDatBaby

The Mountain Man's Babies:

TIMBER

BUCKED

WILDER

HONORED

CHERISHED

BUILT

CHISELED

HOMEWARD

RAISED

FAITHFUL

ABOUT THE AUTHOR

Frankie Love writes filthy-sweet stories about bad boys and mountain men. As a thirty-something mom to six who is ridiculously in love with her own bearded hottie, she believes in love-at-first-sight and happily-ever-afters. She also believes in the power of a quickie.

Find Frankie here:
www.frankielove.net

Made in the USA
Columbia, SC
31 July 2019